SPIKE

BY KATHERINE POTTER

SIMON & SCHUSTER
BOOKS FOR YOUNG READERS
Published by Simon & Schuster, New York
New York   London   Toronto   Sydney   Tokyo   Singapore

SIMON & SCHUSTER BOOKS FOR YOUNG READERS
1230 Avenue of the Americas, New York, New York 10020. Copyright © 1994 by Katherine Potter. All rights reserved including the right of reproduction in whole or in part in any form. SIMON & SCHUSTER BOOKS FOR YOUNG READERS is a trademark of Simon & Schuster. Designed by Lucille Chomowicz. The text for this book is set in 15 point Cochin. The illustrations were done in pastels. Manufactured in the United States of America. 10 9 8 7 6 5 4 3 2 1

Library of Congress Cataloging-in-Publication Data Potter, Katherine. Spike / by Katherine Potter. Summary: Quiet and shy, Jackson is ignored by most people until the day he draws a boy who comes to life and says his name is "Spike." {1. Bashfulness—Fiction. 2. Identity—Fiction. 3. Behavior—Fiction.} I. Title. PZ7.P8524Sp 1994 {E}—dc20 93-11476 CIP
ISBN 0-671-86733-4

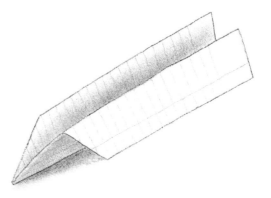

For my husband — KP

Jackson was a quiet little boy, the kind of boy bullies tease, little girls ignore and teachers forget to call on. Shy, his mother called him. "Serious," explained his father. "Jackson who?" asked most people.

Dogs walked right by him;

the school bus sped past his
house without stopping.

His own grandmother kept calling him Jason. But worst of all,
Hazel Smith, who sat at the desk next to his in Mrs. Dumont's class,
never even looked at him.

One day at recess a boy from Jackson's class started telling jokes.
Soon he was surrounded by laughing boys and girls.

Jackson watched from the swings. "If I could make people laugh like
that, I would give up my rare worm collection."

After school Jackson sat at the kitchen table while Cosmo the butler served him milk and gingersnaps.

Suddenly, his father burst into the room. "Hello, my man!" he shouted happily to Cosmo. He hadn't seen Jackson. Out the back door Father banged, not a word to his son.

Jackson sat quietly, staring at the plate of cookies in front of him. He wasn't hungry anymore. He wanted to run after his father, maybe yell at him. But because he was a polite, well-behaved boy, he didn't.

Instead, Jackson went to
his room and started to draw.
First, he drew a big mouth.
Then he drew scribbly hair.
He drew long arms and legs.
He drew big hands and feet.

But Jackson was not pleased with his drawing and began to crumple it up. "I wouldn't do that if I were you," said a voice.

The drawing of a boy peeled right up off the paper and jumped onto the floor. It yawned, stretched, and scratched its scruffy head.

Jackson's mouth was hanging open in disbelief.

"Tryin' to catch flies?" asked the drawing.

Just then Father knocked on the door and came into the room.

"Nice mustache, old man," said the drawing. "Did ya dig it up in the backyard?"

Father looked at his son, frowned, and smiled nervously.

"Pardon me?" he said to Jackson.

"Father," said Jackson. "I drew a picture of a boy, and there he is!" Jackson pointed to the drawing standing next to him.

The drawing smiled and waved. "My name's Spike!" he said.

Father looked where Jackson pointed and said, "There's nothing there, son. And your name most certainly is not Spike."

Father then left the room, stroking his mustache and shaking
his head. "Oh, by the way, dinner is ready," he called back.

Jackson turned to Spike the drawing and shook its hand. "How do you do, my name is Jackson."

Spike jumped up on the bed and lay back. "I know that, egghead!"

Jackson sat next to Spike and whispered excitedly, "I think Father couldn't see you, and yet he heard what you said."

"That's right," replied Spike, "and are we going to have some fun! Let's eat."

At the dinner table Father and Mother were arguing about where to celebrate their wedding anniversary. Mother stopped long enough to ask Jackson, "Would you care for some brussels sprouts, dear?"

"When pigs fly, Ma!" came the reply.

Mother dropped her spoon. "Excuse me?"
she said. "It wasn't me, Mother,"
Jackson said. "Spike said it."

Cosmo the butler passed quietly behind Jackson's chair. "Hey, Cos, how's yer old lady?"

That was enough for Jackson. He grabbed Spike's arm and ran to his room. He put Spike back on the easel, picked up his big pink rubber eraser, and erased Spike's mouth.

The next day at school Spike sat at the desk next to Jackson's, after pushing Hazel Smith out of it.   Hazel shook her fist at Jackson. "You're gonna get it!" she shouted. And then, to Jackson's surprise, she smiled at him.

"It wasn't me!" Jackson said.

Mrs. Dumont, the teacher, called the class to order. "Today, children, we will explore the exciting world of the comma!"

Just then a paper airplane landed on Mrs. Dumont's head.

The class shouted with laughter, and some of the boys patted Jackson on the back.

"Spike did it!" Jackson said.

Poor Jackson was sent to the principal's office.

"Imagine," the principal was saying, "a boy as well behaved as you, acting in this manner."

Suddenly, the principal's toupee flew into the air.

Jackson caught it. He peered up at the principal's angry red face and squeaked, "It was Spike."

Jackson was sent to his room that night. He went straight to the easel and erased Spike's hands. He was just starting on the hair when Cosmo the butler poked his head in.

"By the way, the old lady is very well, thank you," he said.

Next, Jackson erased Spike's nose and ears.

But then Father came into the room. He seemed very puzzled. He walked back and forth. He walked up and down. Then he said, "So what you mean is, you don't like the mustache?"

Jackson looked at his father. Then he looked at the drawing
of Spike, which was not much more than a body and two little eyes.
Spike was quiet. Jackson took a deep breath and said, "Well...it
does look rather...funny." Jackson closed his eyes, waiting for his
father to get mad.

But instead of getting mad, Father smiled. He put his hands on Jackson's shoulders and laughed. Then he hugged Jackson, all the while laughing and laughing.

"What's so funny?" Jackson asked, a little smile on his face.

Father stopped laughing, wiped away a tear, and said, "Whoever this Spike is, tell him I said, thank you."

At dinner that night Jackson made a sculpture out of his mashed potatoes and peas.

Mother said, "You will be a famous artist one day."

When he told Father he was going to marry a girl named Hazel, Father said, "Bring her around to the house. Let's have a look at her."

Jackson kissed and hugged Mother and Father good night and ran up to his room.

Jackson picked up his pencil and drew Spike's feet back in, then his hands, nose, ears, hair, and finally his mouth. In big letters at the bottom of the paper, he signed it JACKSON. Then he taped the drawing to the wall above his desk, where it stays to this day.

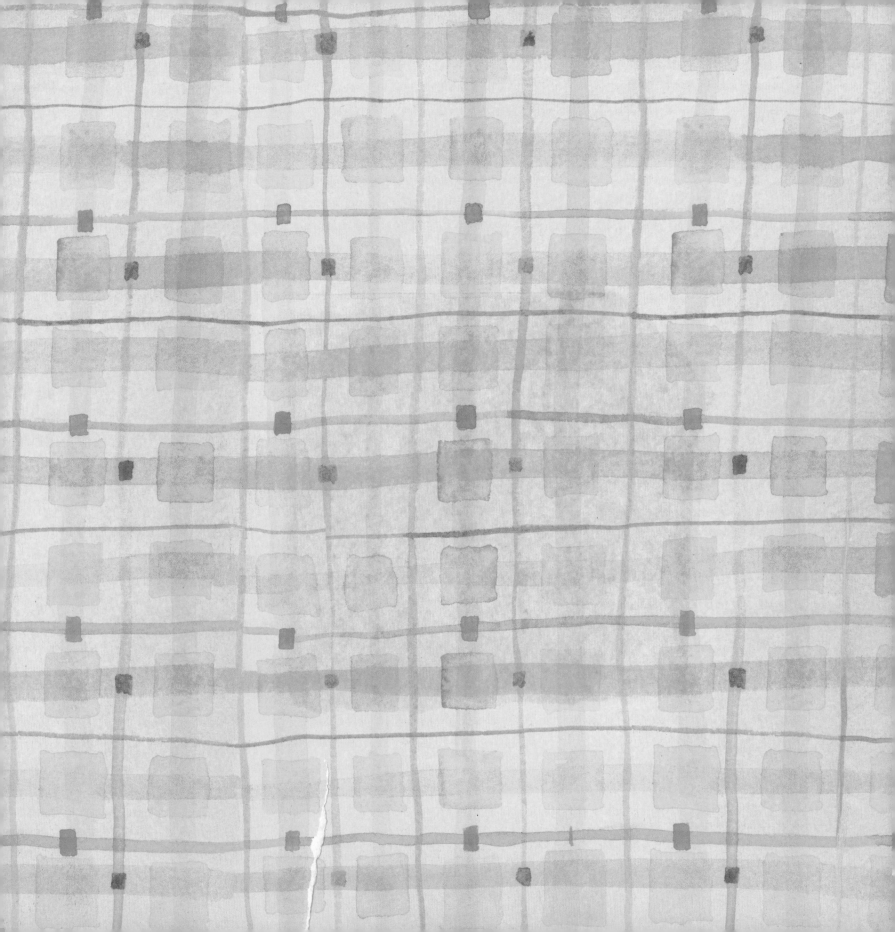

A Farmer's Life for Me

Written by Jan Dobbins

Illustrated by Laura Huliska-Beith

Sung by The Flannery Brothers

Barefoot Books
Step inside a story

Up jump the farmers and set off on their way.

Up jump the children, ready for the day.

Off they go together and this is what they say:

1, 2, 3, it's a farmer's life for me.

It's time for the milking. The cow's named Annabelle.

Careful! She'll kick you and spill the milk as well.

How many buckets are there? Can you tell?

1, 2, 3, it's a farmer's life for me.

We go up to the henhouse, running all the way.

How many warm eggs will we find today?

Pick them up carefully and put them in the tray.

1, 2, 3, it's a farmer's life for me.

Out in the orchard, there blows a summer breeze.

Fat, red cherries are ripening on the trees.

Would you like to eat some? *Mmm!* Yes, please!

1, 2, 3, it's a farmer's life for me.

We're down at the pigsty, peeping through the door
At one mother pig and her family of four.
Can you see the piglets drinking more and more?
1, 2, 3, it's a farmer's life for me.

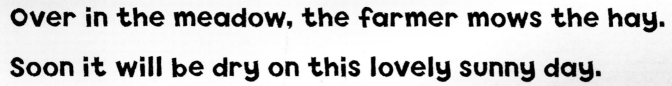

Over in the meadow, the farmer mows the hay.
Soon it will be dry on this lovely sunny day.

Rake it and turn it,

the baler's on its way.

1, 2, 3, it's a farmer's life for me.

Up on the hillside, we're counting lambs and sheep.

Some lambs are lost, though we can hear them bleat.

Rattle the bucket and give them all a treat.

1, 2, 3, it's a farmer's life for me.

Down in the paddock, we check the water trough.

The horses are thirsty; have they got enough?

Turn on the hosepipe. *Whoosh!* Now turn it off.

1, 2, 3, it's a farmer's life for me.

Back in the farmhouse, it's time to make a cake.

Let's get ready so we can start to bake.

Leave it to cool, then slice it into eight.

1, 2, 3, it's a farmer's life for me.

It's time to:

Feed all the ponies and shut the paddock gate.

Close up the henhouse before it gets too late.

The pigs are in the pigsty, the mower's in the shed.

Work's done for the day, and now it's time for bed.
Work's done for the day, and now it's time for bed.

The Working Farm

There are farms all over the world. They are busy places where all sorts of people work to grow food and raise animals. It takes hard work to keep a farm in order. There are different animals to feed and care for, and lots of crops to grow. Some farmers use chemical fertilizers and sprays to help them grow as much food as they can. This is called intensive farming. When farmers use traditional farming methods that are free of chemicals, and let their animals live outside, this is called organic farming.

Milk

Cows, goats and other animals are raised primarily for their milk and meat. When a cow has been milked, the milk is pasteurized, which means it is scalded and strained to make it last longer and to make it safe for drinking and cooking. Milk is full of nutrients like calcium, protein and vitamin D. Dairy foods, such as cheese, butter, yogurt and ice cream, are all made from milk.

Eggs

Many farmers raise chickens, both for their meat and for their eggs. Battery-raised chickens are kept in barns without ever seeing the outdoors or being released from cages. Free-range chickens are allowed to graze outside, stretch their legs and enjoy the fresh air. Eggs are used in all kinds of recipes as well as being delicious on their own.

Cherries

Cherries are a kind of fruit. They are small and round and are grown by farmers in orchards. They are picked when they are juicy and ripe. Some cherries are sour and are used to make pies, jams, juices and smoothies. Other cherries are sweet enough to eat fresh.

Pigs

Pigs are raised by farmers for their meat. Bacon, sausages and pork all come from pigs. Pigskin is used for clothing, bags and horses' saddles.

Hay

In the summer months, many animals eat only grasses. However, in winter they need additional food, like hay. Hay meadows are made up of many different kinds of grasses and wild flowers. Farmers mow their hay meadows once or twice each summer, spread out the hay to dry, then gather it into bales and store it. Hay smells sweet and fragrant!

Sheep

Sheep have thick, woolly coats. In the spring, farmers shear their sheep, clipping off their thick winter wool. The shorn wool is then washed, combed and spun into yarn to make blankets and clothes, or the wool is used to insulate houses. Sheep and lambs are also raised for their meat.

Horses

Before farmers started using tractors and other large machines to do the hard work around the farm, they would use horses to till the fields, and to draw heavy loads by pulling carts and wagons. Nowadays, farmers sometimes use horses to round up cattle and sheep. They also ride them just for pleasure.

A Farmer's Life for Me

Light Fun Swing ♩ = 140

Up jump the farm-ers and set off on their way. Up jump the child-ren, read-y for the day.

Off they go to-geth-er and this is what they say: 1, 2, 3, it's a farm-er's life for me.

Barefoot Books • 294 Banbury Road • Oxford, OX2 7ED
Barefoot Books • 2067 Massachusetts Ave • Cambridge, MA 02140

Text and song copyright © 2013 by Jan Dobbins
Illustrations copyright © 2013 by Laura Huliska-Beith
Musical arrangement copyright © 2013 by The Flannery Brothers
The moral rights of Jan Dobbins and Laura Huliska-Beith have been asserted
Music performed by Mike and Dan Flannery with violins by Jacob Lawson
Recorded, mixed and mastered by Mike Flannery, New York City
Animation by Karrot Animation, London

First published in the United States of America by Barefoot Books, Inc
and in Great Britain by Barefoot Books, Ltd in 2013

Graphic design by Katie Jennings, Nashville, TN
Reproduction by B & P International, Hong Kong
Printed in China on 100% acid-free paper
This book was typeset in Futura T and Spud AF Crisp
The illustrations were painted in gouache and acrylic
on Arches paper, and then digitally collaged

Hardback with enhanced CD ISBN 978-1-84686-790-3
Paperback with enhanced CD ISBN 978-1-84686-791-0
Paperback ISBN 978-1-84686-939-6

British Cataloguing-in-Publication Data:
a catalogue record for this book is available from the British Library
Library of Congress Cataloging-in-Publication Data
is available under LCCN 2012014538

1 3 5 7 9 8 6 4 2